Disney's

THE
LION KING
ZAZU'S VIEW

Adapted by Justine Korman
Illustrated by Josie Yee

A GOLDEN BOOK · NEW YORK
Western Publishing Company, Inc., Racine, Wisconsin 53404

Greetings! Up here! I'm the one with the glossy blue feathers and the long noble bill.

My name is Zazu the hornbill, and I am King Mufasa's right-wing bird. I see everything that happens in the Pride Lands because I've got the bird's-eye view!

Today King Mufasa and Queen Sarabi are presenting their cub, Simba, as a part of the great Circle of Life. All the animals have come to pay their respects to the cub who will one day be the next Lion King. Everyone is here—except the king's jealous brother, Scar.

Unfortunately, Mufasa's rude brother isn't the only problem. The next day I inform His Majesty that the hyenas have been coming into the Pride Lands, where they don't belong.

Mufasa's mane ruffles at the news. "Zazu! Take Simba home," he commands.

Simba wants to help his father turn the hyenas back. But this is no job for a cub barely out of the den.

I wind up cub-sitting Simba as he walks with his young friend Nala. The cubs look so sweet together that before I know it, the plans for their future marriage slip from my beak. But are the lovebirds happy at the news? No!

And who are they mad at? Zazu!

"I can't marry Nala. She's my friend!" Simba shouts at me.

I tell him rules are rules. But Simba says all that will change when he becomes king. And then the whole savannah is rocking as Simba sings about what he'll do as king.

The next thing I know, I'm under several tons of rhinoceros—and Simba and Nala are nowhere in sight! Some days it just isn't worth getting out of the nest.

Of course, wings are better than legs any day, and I soon catch up with the cubs. And where are they? In an elephant graveyard in hyena territory outside the Pride Lands borders!

When I express my concern, Simba doesn't listen.
"I laugh at danger. Ha!" he replies.

His laugh is answered by another. "Hee-hee-hee-hee!"
We're surrounded by hyenas!

I try to use my diplomatic skills to make a hasty exit.
But Simba is too young to know the wisdom of escaping
with all your tail feathers. And if the hyenas have their
way, the cub won't get any older!

And neither will I! The hyenas grab me and march me over to a thermal steam vent. Wow, is that hot! Simba tries to save me, but the hyenas are too much for him.

I'm certain our goose is cooked. Then suddenly Mufasa appears with a mighty *ROAARRRRRR*! With one swoop of his paw, he sends the hyenas flying like a bunch of frightened hens.

But is that enough excitement for the king's cub? Oh, no! The very next day I spot a huge herd of wildebeests on the stampede. And who is in their path? Simba! "I'll fly ahead, Sire," I tell Mufasa.

When I reach Simba, the poor little cub is clinging to a branch. "Zazu! Help me!" he cries.

"Your father is on the way," I assure Simba. "Hold on!"

I fly back to help Mufasa find his son.

"There!" I shriek over the noise of stamping hooves. "On that tree."

Mufasa leaps into the rushing mass of running legs, but I am afraid the wild herd will be too much for one lion—even Mufasa.

"This is terrible!" I squawk. "What am I going to do?" Then I know. "I'll go back for the rest of the pride!"

Suddenly someone swats me from behind. The next thing I know, I'm waking up with an elephant-sized headache. And then things go from bad to far, far worse.

Addressing the pride, Scar announces, "Tragedy has struck. Brave Mufasa and his son, Simba, are gone. With a heavy heart, I must assume the throne."

His next words knock me tail over beak. Scar says his executive staff will be hyenas! Our enemies will now share the Pride Lands!

From my honored position as the king's right-wing bird, I am reduced to singing for my supper. It's that or *be* supper!

Scar is a terrible king. As the years pass under his rule, the Pride Lands dry up. It seems as if the great Circle of Life itself has stopped turning.

Even those flighty hyenas know things can't go on this way.

"There's no food!" they tell King Scar.

Scar blames Sarabi and the lionesses for not hunting well enough.

And then a miracle happens!

Lightning flashes and thunder roars—as loud as
Mufasa himself sounded. A full-grown Simba appears!
He isn't dead. He ran away because Scar lied and told
him he had caused his father's death. Scar was the one
who killed Mufasa, as part of his plot to become king.

And that is all over now! Sarabi and the others fight Scar and his hyenas. Once my cage is smashed, I join the pecking, too. Then, of course, we fly swiftly to victory!

Soon the Pride Lands turn green again. The herds
return. Simba marries Nala. And in time, their son is
brought to Pride Rock to join the great Circle of Life.
And I am here to make sure the future Lion King will
fly straight along the path of his fathers. Because I am
Zazu the hornbill, and that is my job!